The Miracle of Pont-l'Abbé

PUBLISHER'S CHOICE

A COLLECTION OF SLIM VOLUMES
SELECTED BY OUR PUBLISHER

No. 1

The Miracle of Pont-l'Abbé

No one was surprised to learn that Paul-
Antoine had landed his first job at the
biscuiterie of Pont-l'Abbé. After all, monsieur
Martin was well known for his kindness and
his devotion to worthy causes. No, the citizens
of Pont-l'Abbé were startled only by the
political or the symbolic nature of the role
young 'Toine was asked to discharge. Instead of
filling innumerable glass shelves with tins of
biscuits and bottles of local cider and guides to
the cuisine of Brittany in the languages of the
new Europe, the willing youth was offered a

position behind the cash desk alongside monsieur himself. Not handling the money, of course – monsieur Martin hinted that might come later – but helping to greet the esteemed customers and bid them farewell like an apprentice to the post of house manager in any of a dozen respectable provincial theatres of the old school between Quimper and Nantes. Paul-Antoine was even called on in the course of the working day to wrap the various gift items bought by visitors and tourists of every national stripe – the boxes of biscuits and the aprons and tea towels having a regional culinary motif and the ever-popular assortments of Pont-Aven *galettes* that were baked on the premises every day except Sunday.

'May God protect me,' whispered the young man as he neared the famous *biscuiterie* of Pont-l'Abbé on Quai Saint-Laurent just a stone's throw from the port where the desolate forms of the smaller boats rendered redundant by the fish famine were strewn across the muddy basin like the wounded on a field of battle. 'God protect me from LeBrun and Isabel and Daniel the baker boy. Yes, and God bring back the fish –'

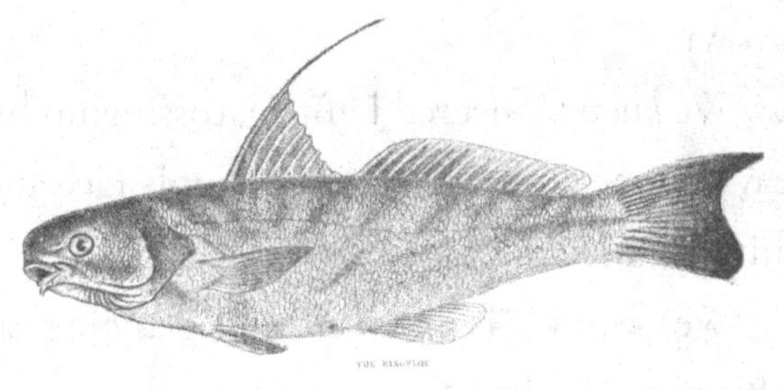

It was only his second week at his job, but already young 'Toine understood he was the focus of an unnatural resentment among his colleagues at the *biscuiterie*. In fact, the new employee had expected trouble, and the pain it brought him, from the moment monsieur Martin had introduced him to the assembled workforce in the short period of calm before last Monday's doors were thrown open on a biscuit-hungry world. 'This is Paul-Antoine,' said monsieur Martin kindly but unnecessarily. It was virtually impossible in Pont-l'Abbé during the dying decades of the old century to come of age without knowing every other kid in town.

'We *knows*,' sneered LeBrun, tossing up his heavy phone with a grin on his pimply face and a hint of menace in his reedy voice.

'We know,' Isabel echoed, glancing at LeBrun and rolling her eyeballs while passing an orange duster between chilblained hands.

'What's the square root of 2,468, swot?' queried Daniel with a sensual glee Paul-Antoine recognised from the school playgrounds of Pont-l'Abbé.

Plainly they were jealous of the upstart in their company. They were jealous of his putative post behind the counter. (Although no specific mention was made of the new recruit's role, everyone very naturally imagined his position of preferment at the right hand of monsieur – there was nowhere else *safe* for the clumsy kid to go.) Of course, they had long envied his extravagant qualities of numerical instinct and statistical insight, his practical feeling for facts, lists, and the mathematical rhythm of life. The youth's curiosity was at once specific and infinite. He loved, for example, the notion of all the tea in China. It was to him no tired figure of speech. He sat for hours pretending to his mother he was lost in a book when in fact he was imagining – no, picturing – all the tea in China. Yes, all of it – every leaf on every sprig of every bush on every terrace in China. People understood that China was composed of paddy fields and terraces. But Paul-Antoine wanted to discover how many terraces and paddy fields there were in China according to the latest census. He wanted to know how many trees he would have to plant today to make up for the carbon dioxide emissions he would be responsible for over his lifetime. (In calculating his projected life span he began with the biblical three score years and ten and then subtracted a number of years in recognition of his special condition – a number he assured himself daily he would reveal to no one.) By far his most challenging project to date was to arrive at a figure for the number of grains of sand on the beach at nearby Penhors. In the winter months, when the moon was at its newest and the tide was at its lowest, the broad beach at Penhors was a wonder. It was quite the nicest thing Paul-Antoine had seen, apart from Brighton Pavilion, of course, which he had visited last year on a school trip to England. As a warm-up exercise before enumerating the particles of sand at Penhors, Paul-Antoine was given to counting and identifying the precious fish that swam more and more sparsely in the waters off Pont-l'Abbé, taking in the Bay of Biscay and the Atlantic Ocean itself from Portugal to Florida and from Canada to Norway. Alongside *all the tea in China* he particularly valued the expression *plenty more fish in the sea.*

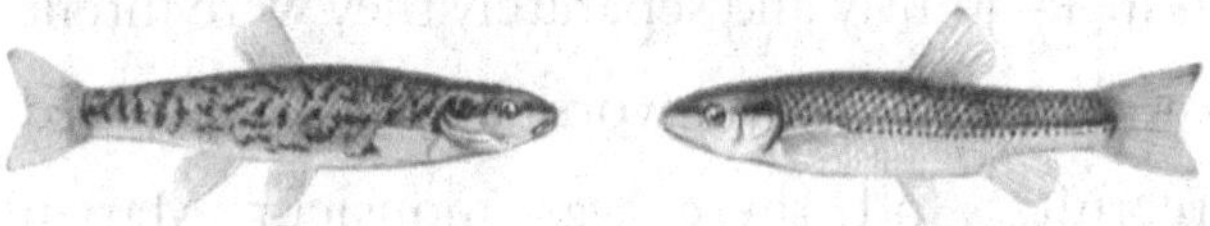

Oh, if only there really were plenty more fish in the sea, he railed, asking God – as he did each night before he fell asleep – to lower the mean temperature just a little in the Gulf of Morbihan so that the shoals might return and the fishermen of Pont-l'Abbé regain their dignity.

'Now, now –' monsieur Martin had cautioned on that first ever Monday with a gentle note of reproach. 'I'm not sure 2,468 is even a perfect square or square number, Daniel.'

And thus was the pattern established. There was Paul-Antoine, permanent provocation to his peers. (The term is the most generous available, for he had no friends.) There were his colleagues LeBrun, Daniel and Isabel – jointly and separately they were intent on doing their level worst by the unpractised recruit. And there was monsieur Martin himself, ever ready with a quiet word of encouragement or a constructive rebuke. '*Absolument pas*, young man – I have to insist again you take Napoléon home to madame Billiet immediately, the better to focus on your duties here.'

This was on the second day of the first week of 'Toine's employ. 'But monsieur –' stammered the apprentice wrapper of gifts, coiling and uncoiling the leather dog leash behind his back.

'*Pas de mais*, my friend – no *buts*. It is simply not done in this day and age to introduce a beagle or any other beast into your place of work – especially when that place is also a repository of the freshest comestibles and the finest souvenirs. Now, go, *tout de suite*.' That the owner of the most famous *biscuiterie* in Finistère had a soft spot for Paul-Antoine was not generally known in the environs. Even later, when the sad affair was concluded and the statue commemorating Paul-Antoine had been unveiled and hurriedly consecrated at Quai Saint-Laurent by the mayor of Pont-l'Abbé and a priest, the kindly retailer's true role and interest were not widely recognised.

*

It was around his third or fourth week at the *biscuiterie* that Paul-Antoine noticed a shift in the pattern and texture of his close relationship with the sea – with the sea and all the fish in it. It struck the young man with the

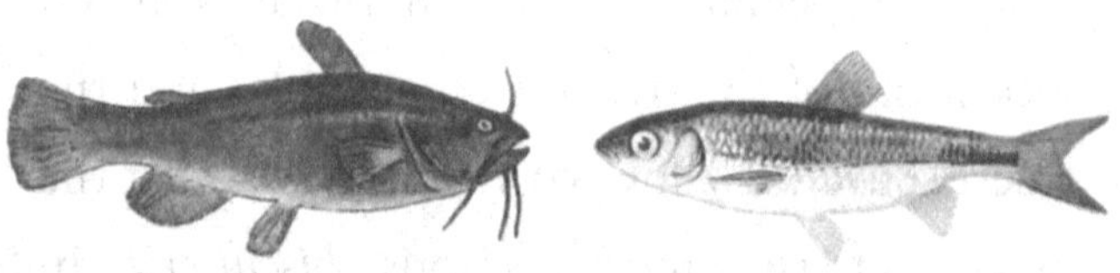

force of a blow. It had the inevitability of a calling or a destiny. It had the insistence of the moon on the fate of the tide at Penhors. From now on, everything would be different. For example, there was the change, recognised first at five past nine on an otherwise ordinary Tuesday, in Isabel's attitude towards him. Might he yet be mistaken? No. As he took up his customary position behind the cash desk and watched monsieur Martin break the early fruits of Daniel's ovens into bite-sized morsels with which to tempt the day's peckish first customers, Paul-Antoine had a clear sense of it. She was lingering – there was no other way to describe it – in a region of the shop directly in front of the till, her chilblained hand coming and going with a fluent economy among the busy shelves, her tangerine duster darting speculatively back and forth across the aisle. On the one side she had the popular *galette* assortments in their highly decorative tins – it was a source of satisfaction to monsieur, quiet aesthete and democrat, that even the slightest of the artists of Gauguin's celebrated circle of Pont-Aven advertised representative work on the lids of those tins – and on the other a tiered carousel stocked all around with freshly baked biscuits *de la maison* of cocoa nut, chocolate, lemons, oranges, almonds, butter, eggs and sugar in every combination. Behind her were the calendars and diaries with an obvious coastal theme, plus the goblets etched with lighthouses of the Brittany peninsula, and the souvenir crockery and the aprons and the tea towels harking back to a halcyon era, an era of marine plenty invoked marvellously in needlepoint illustration by fish of the shoreline and fish of the ocean – fish manifold, mythic,

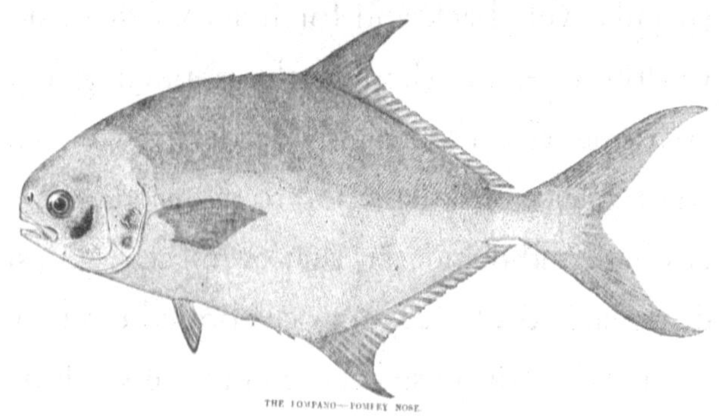

THE POMPANO—POMFRET NOSE.

wonderful. Suddenly she smiled at him. Isabel flashed a smile at the cash desk, at its most recent champion. Really, there could be no doubt. And for Paul-Antoine it was an epiphanic moment of revelation, a kind of watershed. Madame Billiet aside, no girl and no woman had ever smiled at him in that wide open way before.

A fat Belgian customer approached the cash desk with his wife and children behind him and, in front and aloft, two bottles of pure juice cider of the region. 'Is it local, the cider? I mean – I absolutely must have cider from the region spanning Brittany and Normandy, which is one of France's principal apple-growing areas.'

'Ah, yes – I see sir understands something of the geography of cider production in our bountiful country. Let me assure sir that –'

Here, monsieur's courtesies were interrupted by a voice, calm and resolute, from behind him. 'Our apples are harvested between September and December, then crushed and pressed in January. Winter's cold slows down fermentation, which can last up to three months, or ninety days, or 2,160 hours, or 129,600 minutes, or –'

'Let us pause for reflection there, 'Toine –' This last thoughtful suggestion came from monsieur as he received two bottles of cider across the counter and prepared to ring up the sale at the till.

'No, no –' said the Belgian customer's wife. 'Let the young man speak. After all – how can we weigh up the next generation's worth if we fail to invite their opinion or entertain their point of view?'

'Just so, madame,' said monsieur Martin. 'My sentiments –'

'You see – sweet cider has an alcohol content of between two and a half and three per cent,' interjected Paul-Antoine, voice rising steadily in volume while gaining rapidly in tempo. 'In other words, roughly the same proportion as current fish stocks in the depleted Gulf of Morbihan account for as a percentage of the old stocks.'

'Fascinating –' adjudged the wife of the chubby Belgian. 'Quite, quite fascinating.'

'But what would madame sacrifice to restore the fish stocks to our bay?' It just popped out. Of course, Paul-Antoine didn't mean to hold her *personally* responsible for local maritime conditions. He was speaking, rather, in more general terms. An unusual silence set in, awkward but attentive. It was another turning point, admitted monsieur Martin to himself afterwards – a key moment in the affair.

'Madame's interest is most gratifying,' interposed the biscuit mogul smoothly, ever protective of his young charge.

But for Paul-Antoine it was already too late. He gathered in the two cider bottles expertly gift-wrapped by monsieur. He let one slip. It must have been her condescending smile, delivered hard on the heels of Isabel's own, which unnerved him. 'Most local cider is like champagne, madame –' he blurted out finally, eyeballs rolling up behind his eyelids. 'It comes in corked bottles.'

And when he came round several seconds later in a puddle of the fermented juice, Isabel was there with monsieur to help him up. 'You're odd,' she advised approvingly, leading him to a secret place behind the recipe books in English, Spanish, Polish and German.

'You mean crazy, don't you?' Paul-Antoine said.

'I mean special. Weird beats normal any day of the week.'

Could he trust her? He didn't contradict her.

'Like the game,' she went on.

Again, he didn't say anything.

'You know –' she persisted. 'When scissors cut paper and stone blunts scissors and paper wraps stone.' And saying that she lifted up his hands and wrapped them in her own hands so red and raw, and he almost passed out all over again in the face of her attentions. He had the idea he might pay with his life for such partisanship. Later, rallying behind the cash desk and insisting to monsieur Martin he would work the full balance of the day, Paul-Antoine bade farewell to certain English shoppers with a clearer commitment to consumer satisfaction in his heart and two novel imperatives in his head. Yes, from today he would embark on a practical project to catalogue the human smile in all its guises. It

was a matter of self-preservation, he decided –
nothing more or less. And he would strive to
rid himself of the siren voice of the ocean, so
damaging lately to the quality of ordinary
interpersonal relationships.

'*Au revoir*,' said the English shoppers. '*Au
revoir et bonne journée.*'

'*Bonne journée à vous*,' said Paul-Antoine,
congratulating himself on his new customer
focus. 'May your nets be heavy –'

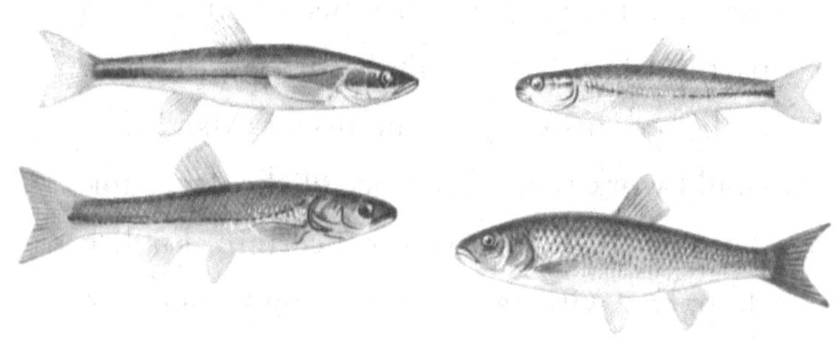

Once again, it just slipped out. But this
time, noted monsieur with the quiet alarm that
came to typify his response to significant

24

developments, there was at least one important difference. It was in the voice. Not only was the voice subtly changed from the youth's own. Worse, it seemed Paul-Antoine couldn't himself hear it. It was as if someone, or something, had taken possession of his speech.

'I beg your pardon?' said a shopper, bearing off a tin of biscuits decorated handsomely in a post-impressionist style. 'What did you say, young man?'

'May your nets be heavy. May your seas be full –'

*

As the fish famine endured, an atmosphere of crisis hung more and more noticeably over the once proud port of Pont-l'Abbé. No one was unaffected.

'I'm rather worried about the lad,' admitted monsieur Martin, turning to confront madame Billiet behind the trestle table of her Sunday stall in place de la République.

Week by week the market grew meaner and its produce more meagre until it seemed that the very lifeblood had been sucked out of the community along with its fish. 'Might as well pack up early today,' said madame, arranging and rearranging the shortbreads – rejects of the town's famous *biscuiterie* – on the table. 'It appears man cannot live by your cookies alone, my darling.'

'Did you hear me, Mathilde?'

'I heard you, yes –'

'But haven't you witnessed it for yourself? He has developed a dangerous obsession with the sea and all the fish in it.'

'With the few that remain, you mean.'

'Mathilde – the boy is speaking in tongues.'

'Dear Martin – the boy is special. He has

always been special. Have you ever doubted it? Our son –'

'Sssh, Mathilde,' urged monsieur, glancing over his shoulder at the darkening square. His was a protective instinct honed in silence and in secret over sixteen summers – all the years of the boy's life. It was an instinct that glowed fiercely in monsieur's heart from day to day and from hour to hour. How it warmed him in the presence of cold nights. How it comforted him in the face of his loneliness. It didn't exist, his love for the boy and the boy's mother, which were one and the same. It went undeclared to a self-satisfied world – it had to. Nevertheless, it burned in the dark. It was as nothing. It was everything. It burned with the same fire today as on the first night at Penhors. It shone with the same light as the moon above Penhors beach, that gorgeous expanse broader than the broadest highway. Monsieur recalled the scenario now with the intensity of a recurring dream. The moon was waxing rapidly. The tide pushed higher and higher towards the uppermost ribbon of sand in the shadow of the road. There was the narrow strip, cool and dry and shiny with tiny shells. It was here they lay down together for the first and last time and conceived their secret love. Sixteen years ago! He remembered it as if it had been yesterday, or the day before that.

'What shall we do, Martin?'

He looked at her now in the deserted marketplace and saw the light in her eye that would soon go out. 'I don't know, my love,' he acknowledged candidly. 'I just don't know –'

*

It was natural that the exposed strand at Penhors should be a favourite of Sunday kite

28

enthusiasts old and young during the hours of leisure following church. Paul-Antoine walked further and further from their colourful presence with his fishing rod over his shoulder and Napoléon at his heel. Dog and master splashed side by side through the big puddles left by the retreating tide until they reached a spot where they were alone with sea and sky.

'This is the place, my friend,' confirmed Paul-Antoine, setting his sack down on a sandy spit towards the upper limit of the surf. It was an experiment. That was how he viewed it. There was a feeling inside him he just couldn't ignore. He didn't know how to describe it. He didn't know what it was if not the call of the ocean or the pull of the tide. He took down his rod and cast the weight at the horizon and waited for a few moments only before bringing in his line. He used no bait – nothing. He had the conviction, overwhelming and irresistible, that he needed none. His faithful hound was barking at the sea. Yes, Napoléon could sense it too. It was true – it was a true feeling. As he lifted the line from the surf Paul-Antoine saw

the first fish flap in the low sun. The fish was on the beach now, gleaming and flapping. Master and dog ran back through the shallow pools with here and there a starfish or a razor shell on the sand until they regained the kites and the road. They hitched a ride as far as Pont-l'Abbé. By the time they reached the marketplace the daylight was fading fast and the stallholders were packing up their wares. Paul-Antoine saw his mother, alone behind her table. She waved at him and smiled, and he felt his heart jump like a salmon, and when he emptied six gleaming fish from his sack onto the table he heard her give a little cry of wonder tinged with dread.

'Did I do something wrong, mama?' he asked her, and he heard Napoléon let out a whimper under the table.

'What's happening, 'Toine?' she whispered, her fingers pressed to her mouth. 'I don't know what's happening to us any more.'

*

Paul-Antoine's last day at work began in much the same way as all the other days. Daniel

31

and LeBrun confronted him at the earliest opportunity.

'Ready to sing today, little sparrow?' said Daniel, pinning Paul-Antoine to the floor of the bakery with his knees.

'Just tell us where you gets 'em from,' demanded LeBrun from above. 'Then we'll leave you alone, freak of nature – *forever.*'

For some weeks now madame Billiet's Sunday market stall had been the talk of all Finistère. People came to place de la République just to look, waiting resentfully in line for a glimpse of the fresh fish spread plump and plentiful on the trestle table. As the days passed by and a measure of unwelcome celebrity began to attend madame, there was even the suggestion, dismissed by the modest widow on a friend's advice, of police protection. Tongues wagged, spiteful and covetous, at the confessionals and supper tables of Pont-l'Abbé. But try as the local press might to locate her sources, madame spurned all inducements to share them.

'Your mother's a witch, so she is.'

'Look how much she bloody charges for them fishes –'

'Just tell us where you get them from, freak-show.'

From the sea, of course, you assholes.

'Tell us what you know –'

'If you knows what's good for you.'

And so it went on with a kind of fateful rhythm. And with every hissed injunction came another blow. 'Why don't you make it easy on yourself?' Daniel pleaded finally.

'God knows we don't want to hurt you *proper*,' LeBrun said.

'No, wait,' cried Isabel from the other side of the hatch.

It was already too late. Paul-Antoine

looked up at her from his prone position on the floor. What he wanted most at that moment was to see her smile again – the way she smiled all those weeks ago. As his eyeballs rolled up in their sockets he began to declaim in a voice unrecognisable as his own. One by one and species by species he brought forth a roll-call of fish – fish of the shoreline and fish of the deeper sea from the Gulf of Morbihan to the Bay of Biscay and the Atlantic Ocean itself.

'*Bar, mulet, talan, requin –*'

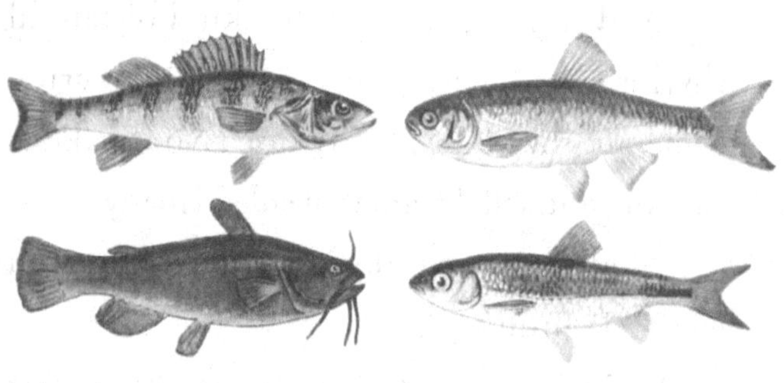

Daniel leapt up. He backed away alongside LeBrun.

'Rouget, touille, maquereau, sardine, vieille, maigre, daurade, aiguille, raie, sole, rousette, torpille, vive, turbot, orphie, anguille, congre, seiche,

lieu, saumon, truite, homard, araignée, tourteau, etrille, crevette, huitre, moule, palourde, pétoncie, coque, praire, couteau –' Still the dreadful litany went on.

'Fetch monsieur,' cried Daniel at last.

'*Now* –' added LeBrun urgently.

'He isn't here,' Isabel complained.

'Then go and find him.'

'Phone him. No – call madame Billiet.'

This much was a matter of police record. When the inglorious affair was investigated Isabel gave a true account of events up until the moment she ran from the biscuit shop to fetch madame Billiet. For a further history the authorities and those close to Paul-Antoine were obliged to rely on the confused and contradictory testimonies of the two principal witnesses. It was unfortunate that the one had developed in a matter of just a few swift hours the most debilitating stammer. The other, meanwhile, was unable to hold the eye having been afflicted in the shortest possible time by squints of an appalling severity. Two key elements of the case were incontrovertible –

the sudden and miraculous manifestation of fish within Pont-l'Abbé's harbour as the tide ebbed rapidly away, and the similarly rapid rise towards a flood mark just below the ceiling of sea water inside the town's famous *biscuiterie*.

It was as if the shop filled up as the harbour emptied. Paul-Antoine was riding on the water. As the waters rose, he rose with them, surrounded by bobbing biscuit tins and clinking bottles of finest Brittany cider.

'B-b-black magic, it was, and n-n-no mistake,' insisted Daniel, smacking his forehead and jaw repeatedly according to a complex but random remedial regime.

'No – he weren't speaking to us no more,' added LeBrun, eyes peering in two quite different directions on either side of monsieur. 'That's because all the sea water were pouring out of his mouth like there were no tomorrow.'

*

Although the autopsy discovered no liquid on the lung, the coroner declared Paul-Antoine dead from asphyxia consistent with a drowning

38

at sea. For sixteen days and nights the inexplicably low tides left the muddy floor of Pont-l'Abbé's harbour strewn with flapping fish of every species.

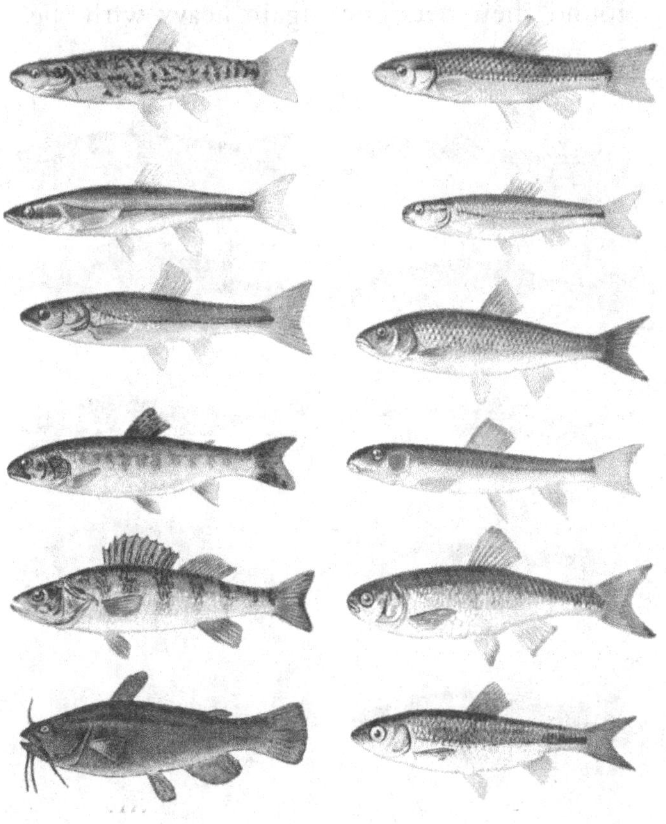

On the seventeenth day no fish were left stranded on the mud. The tides came and went under the usual influence of the moon. And from that day the proud fishermen of the town found their nets once again heavy with the local catch.

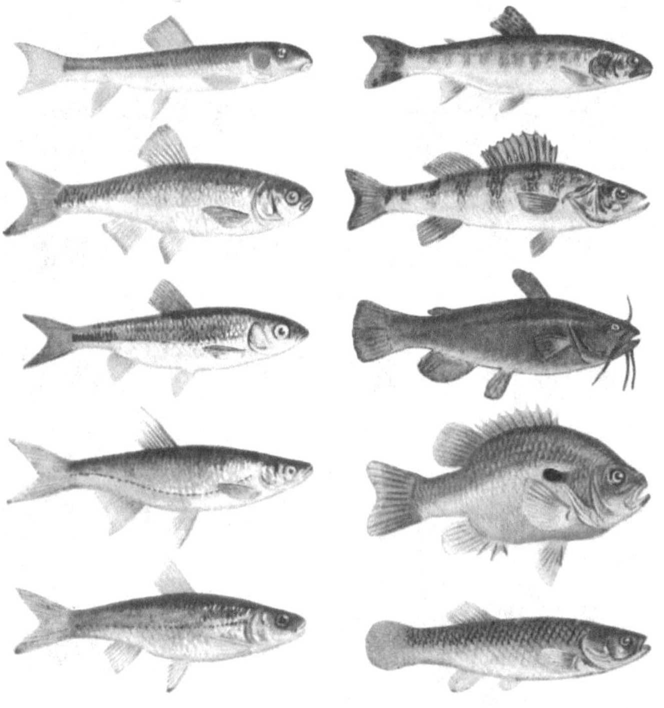

The citizens of Pont-l'Abbé wasted no time in commissioning a statue to commemorate Paul-Antoine. The winning proposal was selected for its ingenuity in surmounting a technical challenge – a challenge associated with raising the sculpted likeness into the air above a notional flood. There was a further call to arrive at a fitting inscription to grace the commissioned piece. When at last the statue was unveiled at Quai Saint-Laurent by the town's mayor a murmur of appreciation ran round the dignified assembly. Smiling radiantly on life, Paul-Antoine rose effortlessly above the plinth by virtue of a reinforced leash linking his right hand to the collar of his dog.

Daniel and LeBrun disappeared from view in the best interests of public order and for their own safety. Isabel went to Nantes and began a new life there as a dental hygienist. Madame Billiet made a solemn pilgrimage every Sunday from the Sacred Heart convent at Quimper in order to lay flowers at the statue in Pont-l'Abbé. Of those closest to Paul-Antoine only monsieur Martin drew strength from the affair. His *biscuiterie* continued to flourish on the same site a stone's throw from the harbour. Every day as he passed the statue honouring his secret son he stopped, a beagle by his side, to review the legend on the plinth. After all, he had penned it. *I am ordinary. I am the same as everyone else. No, wait – I am special. I am like you.*

Barry Stewart Hunter

BORN IN ADEN, BARRY STEWART HUNTER
GREW UP IN THE MIDDLE EAST AND SCOTLAND.
A NOVELIST, SHORT STORY WRITER AND SCREENWRITER,
HE LIVES IN LONDON.

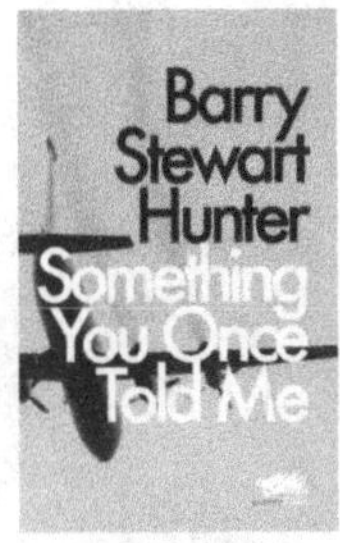

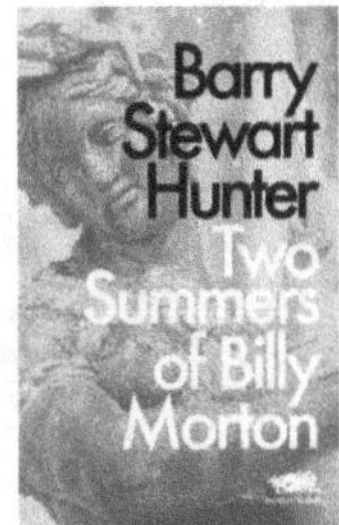

THE CAMBRIDGE QUEER PRESS PUBLISHES A UNIFORM EDITION
OF BARRY STEWART HUNTER'S MAJOR FICTION WORKS:
*SOMETHING YOU ONCE TOLD ME, ADEN, TWO SUMMERS OF BILLY MORTON,
THE SWIMMING OF THE DEER, REPUBLIC OF NORTH LONDON*
AND *STORIES FOR BOYS* (IN WHICH *THE MIRACLE OF PONT-L'ABBÉ*
FIRST APPEARED).

WWW.CAMBRIDGEQUEERPRESS.CO.UK

PUBLISHER'S CHOICE

A COLLECTION OF SLIM VOLUMES
SELECTED BY OUR PUBLISHER

No. 1

THE MIRACLE OF PONT-L'ABBÉ
A SHORT STORY FROM THE COLLECTION
STORIES FOR BOYS
BY BARRY STEWART HUNTER

No. 2

THE FIRST MANIFESTO OF SURREALISM
THE STORY OF YVAN GOLL'S MANIFESTO OF SURREALISM
PUBLISHED 14 DAYS BEFORE ANDRÉ BRETON'S
WITH AN ESSAY BY MARTIN FIRRELL

No. 3

OUT OF WATER
A QUEER HORROR STORY FROM THE COLLECTION
SHAPES IN THE DARK
BY WILLIAM JACKSON

No. 4

150 YEARS OF GERTRUDE STEIN
OUR PUBLISHER'S CHOICE FROM THE SHORT
WORKS OF GERTRUDE STEIN TO MARK
150 YEARS SINCE HER BIRTH

No. 5

ALL THE BEAUTIFUL BOYS
AN ORIGINAL SHORT STORY FROM
THE MASTER OF QUEER BRITISH
HORROR, WILLIAM JACKSON

No. 6

HOW TO WRITE LIKE MRS WOOLF
C. FARR ON HOW A WRITER
MIGHT SET OUT TO CREATE
RATHER THAN IMITATE FORM